From Light to Dark and Back Again

From Light to Dark and Back Again

by Allison Symes

Chapeltown Books

British Library Cataloguing in Publication Data

A Record of this Publication is available from the British Library

ISBN 978-1-910542-06-4

This edition published 2017 by Chapeltown Books
Manchester, England

All Chapeltown books are published on paper derived from sustainable
resources.

Contents

INTRODUCTION

This is a collection of my flash fiction pieces. The tones vary from humorous to dark and back again but all reflect my style of fiction. Some have appeared on Cafélit (http://cafelit.co.uk) and others on Shortbread Short Stories. The latter are some of the very first pieces I wrote years ago, Cafélit is more recent and other stories are brand new for this collection.

Sometimes I will put up a flash fiction piece on my Fairytales with Bite website (www.fairytaleswithbite.weebly.com). I share writing tips on my Allison Symes – This World and Others website (www.allisonsymes-thisworldandothers.weebly.com).

I also write about writing, books and stories and interview authors on Chandler's Ford Today, an online magazine where I blog weekly. See www.chandlersfordtoday.allisonsymes

My favourite authors are Terry Pratchett, Jane Austen and P.G. Wodehouse but I also like reading crime, historical fiction and non-fiction amongst other genres. I'm a member of the Society of Authors and Association of Christian Writers.

I hope you enjoy the stories.

JOB VACANCY

Wanted: Wizard's Assistant. Must not meddle with equipment, books or anything that replicates, especially cleaning materials. The right candidate will enjoy a generous salary, interesting travel and a long, healthy life. Candidates must apply to Brankaresh c/o the Creepy Mansion on the Hill at Hanging in the Oaks.

This time, Brankaresh thought, I'll get an assistant who doesn't skimp on the cleaning by using magic. The castle took weeks to dry out properly last time. And I'd like to stop having to clear up the mess caused by blasting impudent idiots apart...

Why should I have the bad name?

A KIND OF HELL

I never believed in hell. Of all my mistakes in life, I never thought that would be my biggest. But it is.

There are no flames. There's no smell of sulphur. I am surrounded by furry animals of differing sizes. So where is the problem?

Not only am I allergic to fur so I spend most of my time sneezing my head off, I spent my time on Earth shooting furry animals. Not with a camera either. Somehow I thought hunting animals only for fun was macho.

Guess who are holding the guns now?

JOB SATISFACTION

Thud!

The fairy returned to what she'd wrongly sworn was an open window.

Damn! Every bloody window was shut. Her scowl curdled the street's milk. She fired a spell at the letterbox to keep it open. Many fairies narrowly escaped being sliced in half by a clanging letterbox but nobody cheated her of an overdue incisor yet alone a snoring bully…

Outside her client's bedroom, the fairy rummaged through her pockets. When humans made her work harder than necessary, she returned the compliment. The fairy grinned at her pliers. There were times she really loved her job.

COLLECTOR'S PIECE

In the smiling man's cabinet was a bottle containing a cursing, pink-clothed fairy, surrounded by multi-coloured bottles stuffed with creatures that lived once.

Alas no fairy could grant their own wishes...

At midnight, the bottles were smashed, exhibits scattered and the fairy hugged by her khaki wearing friends. The boss wanted to console her. While knowing he wanted sex (he'd eyed up her wings for ages), she asked for something all fairies understood.

In the restored cabinet next day, a big central bottle contained the shrunken figure of a horrified looking man.

And the fairies laughed.

GRATITUDE

'Found it?' Lily, a water nymph, watched Flo leave the lake.

Scowling, Flo held up the sword she'd sought for six hours. Lily waited for the explosion. When Flo was peeved, she swore. In their magical environment the uncouth Flo turned the air purple but she was the expert on retrieving mysterious magical objects.

'Not before bloody time. We must force the bloody humans to return this so why let them borrow it? The boss can shove the bloody thing in a marble block. Let some sodding human retrieve it from that! That should bloody stuff them.'

SHOPLIFTING

The boots were missing again, the fifth theft this week.

There were cameras, enough staff to serve customers and act as minders. Sandra herself was always around. Someone had it in for her. They must do.

Sandra adjusted her hold-up stocking. Tucked into the top was a wand. She was a magical novice but even she could transform matter, as her mysterious thief would soon discover.

Sandra smiled. She didn't start life as a fairy. She knew abductions were wrong but couldn't change her past so she'd just make the best of it instead.

EVERY LITTLE DETAIL

The calligraphy on the long list was stunning. The reader was relieved he never produced it. That was his senior assistants' work and kept them out of his white hair. This was as well given they were notorious for mischief making. He needed that now as much as an allergy to mince pies and sherry.

Given the reader's role was to check the list (twice, mind you), he had enough to do without chastising his elves in the run up to Christmas Eve. And Ofpole was due next week. High standards must be sustained. Nobody liked a bad inspection report. Even Santa.

LEARNING THE TRADE

I read the master's books. I pronounced the right words correctly. I'd heard him often enough so knew where to put the emphasis to trigger the magic. He said I'd learn a lot – and I did. Now I'm out on my ear and told I'm lucky to live *and* remain in my original form.

What went wrong?

I cast a quick cleaning charm and couldn't make it stop. You'd have thought taking on apprentices and knowing we're all a curious bunch, Master would have a stop charm in his Big Book of Spells but no…

JUMPING THROUGH HOOPS

He didn't lie, I'll give him that. He put on a circus all right and he was cheap. Claimed his show entertained all ages. He didn't mention its side effects though.

Next time I look for a children's entertainer I shall ask searching questions. I felt a fool when I realised what kind of circus the chap was "running". It took hours for me to sort the house out properly.

My poor collie certainly doesn't want the circus back. The only ones who enjoyed the party were the bloody fleas, the "stars" of the show.

LITTLE PACKAGES

I've lived with the teasing all my life but now and then I tire of it and take myself off somewhere for a break from those who think I need jokes made about my "condition" the whole time.

Given sexism, racism and anti-ginger jokes are rightly condemned, when will discrimination on grounds of height stop? If I hear the words "good things come in little packages" one more time, I tell you I will scream.

Sorry, I'm getting wound up again. Time for another retreat then. Excuse me. I'm just off through the cat flap…

THE TRUTH

What they said everyone knew was untrue so why did they still lie?

Of course there was no such thing as a flying saucer. Nor had any landed on the village green. What had landed there was a Mark 3 Intergalactic Spacecraft with the latest time warp technology and it flew like a dream.

If you're going to invade a planet, you do it properly. You have the right equipment, everything from the most sophisticated laser weapons to a machine that could travel through time and space.

Flying saucers? Really!

Sometimes Becram wondered why his people bothered with Planet Earth.

THEY DON'T UNDERSTAND

I told Belinda, my carer, it was partly my fault. She didn't understand. Said I was punishing myself. I'm not. My Joan would've understood though I can hear her telling me not to be bloody silly. My beautiful, lively Joan left me yesterday.

Joan and I lived in neighbouring streets as kids. We dodged Hitler's bombs. We crammed in down the Tube with our families. After the war, we grew up, dated, faced the austerity era and married once we had enough coupons. Joan wanted to look her best. She always did. Damn her, she even did so yesterday. Of all the times she could have let it go... no, she had to have her makeup, her best dress, her Tweed by Yardley scent...

Joan and I had one child, Simon, who, aged eight, was mown down by a drunk driver. They didn't worry about drink driving then. Had it been a politician's child, the limit would have come in sooner than 1967. Politicians don't change. Same bloody patronizing attitude to us peasants. Worse, if I'd been home on time that night, as I should've been, Simon wouldn't have sneaked out of the house to find me. Joan kept saying that wasn't my fault, it's what kids do but I never did believe her. She was being kind, that was all.

As for the miscarriages, Joan would've kept trying but I couldn't bear to see her go through more pain. Each miscarriage weakened her. I felt guilty. I urged her to let it go, relax, make a new life, take up interests. I helped. I should be proud. It did take her mind off some of her troubles but right now the last thing I am is proud.

Joan said we were lucky. We survived the war. Anything after that was a bonus. She was unlucky to have a stupid husband. I helped her relax all right. I got Joan smoking. I lit her first cigarette.

The lung cancer got her yesterday.

CALLING THE DOCTOR

I shouldn't have put it off but I never liked calling the doctor out unnecessarily. Besides if you can't afford it, you make do.

Still I've found a nice doctor who is calling later. I haven't long now. All my fault but he says he can ease my pain, he'll be only too pleased to sort everything out and I needn't worry about what happens to my body. That's good. All my family died before me, see, so I'm glad he's taking care of that.

His name? Odd one, I know, but it is Doctor Frankenstein.

SERVING UP A TREAT

I learned ages ago not arguing saved many beatings. Calming things down generally worked. But not last time.

Looking back, I think he must've been on something. He was more aggressive than usual (as if I needed that!) and was spoiling for a fight. My policy of not letting him have one, my appeasement, failed. He'd picked up the solid wooden chair to beat me with when I did something unexpected.

I put on the table my home made banoffee pie, his favourite. This one was special.

He never got to take a second mouthful.

SEEING THE LIGHT

I remember the noise and then it went blissfully quiet. I heard people screaming but I didn't know what they were on about. Nor did I care to find out. The pain suddenly went too.

Now I see a wonderful light. It feels as if something is wanting to pull me away from this light. I don't know why. It is beautiful. Warmth emanates from it. I want to sink into that warmth.

Besides it seems a struggle to go back to where I came from. I am tired. I want everything to stop.

WATCHING MYSELF

Experiments happen. Experiments go wrong. Anyway, much scientific progress has been made due to mistakes. The best lessons come from discovering what you *don't* do.

I know – in my case it's dangerous. But I *didn't* know when I began. I thought only I would be affected.

I *am* doing all I can to ensure others aren't endangered. I can't do more. I *have* destroyed the rest of that potion as you call it, chemical formula as I think of it.

If you'll pardon the expression, there really will only be one Dr Jekyll and Mr Hyde.

TIME FOR TEA

Horace finished arranging the tea things. Ellen and James were due.

It was a year since his children's last visit. He'd bought their favourite edibles – a Battenberg cake, a Victoria sponge, jam tarts, iced buns and mini doughnuts. The sandwiches were filled with either a cheese and onion spread or prawn mayonnaise filler. His finest crockery and silver tea pot were on his mahogany table.

Pity they don't do their best by me, he thought. *They're well married, earn lots, own homes so why keep writing, urging me to be careful with my money? Are they that eager for their inheritance?*

Susie, his friend, said she'd always made Ellen and James welcome so there was no need for them to stop visiting. All Susie could think was perhaps they had worries and needed time to tackle them or didn't want to bother him. Susie said she'd take that attitude if she was lucky enough to have a spouse and family. You would want the family to have family time, Susie said, and was she getting in the way? Maybe Ellen and James felt she was. Horace refuted that. He'd sworn a lot, teaching his children several new words in the process, but it cheered Susie and after that Ellen and James stopped visiting.

Horace stared at the Victoria sponge. After today Ellen and James wouldn't worry any more. It was the least he could do. He should've thought of it before.

Horace would have that wonderful coffee Susie made with his cakes and sandwiches. His children drank tea. They'd need something nice to recover from being told they could forget any inheritance.

Susie was right. Best to have tea first. It was sweet of her to worry he'd get upset. The doctors would be pleased at her concern given Horace's heart was failing. He wasn't telling Ellen and James that. They'd lost any right to know for abandoning him. They should've known after a short interval they were to come back and apologise for being rude about Susie. He'd told them what to do. They'd ignored him.

Horace looked at the blonde in the opposite armchair. Susie was there for him after his illness. His children were not. Susie said she'd begged them to return, but they hadn't phoned or visited. Doubtless they'd assumed he'd die. Horace assumed they'd have good excuses. They'd make sure. He'd hear them over tea, no doubt, but it was too late for that.

No, Horace thought, *Susie gets the money. It was good of her to tell me how much poison to put in the tea.* It's funny the things you find out, Susie told him. *Susie knows the ways of the world. She'll guide me, not use me unlike some I could name.*

My children will say goodbye to me after all. It just won't be how they expect, he thought, *though it will be what they deserve.*

TRIPPING THE LIGHT FANTASTIC

Jenny Simmons danced gracefully. She was one of my best and most hard-working pupils. I can't say that for all I've tried to teach.

Dancing is hard work and good exercise. Jenny told me she wanted to get her weight down and, as well as dieting, thought if she could find a fun exercise she was more likely to stick with it. It worked for her. Over the months her weight did drop.

Then it went wrong.

Now when she trips the light fantastic, she *trips*.

Jenny Simmons had a stroke. She is 48.

PUNISH THE INNOCENT

Dear Sarah,

They say, the perfect crime is where the criminal doesn't get caught. Wrong. It's where nobody realises a crime took place. I know. I've done it. It's the perfect way to avenge my son, your brother.

Why should some rat get away with murder for using a weapon which isn't even considered as one? Forget sodding James Bond. Every bloody driver has a licence to kill. They just don't realise it.

Poor David did, when he lay dying on Applebury High Street, thanks to some boozy fool. The driver didn't see those big black and white stripes indicating a zebra crossing or the poles with the flashing yellow bulbs, let alone the young man carefully following my advice, to find a safe place to cross. Safe! Ha!

As you read this you'll know that I'm dead but so will that b— who killed your brother. There's a pleasing symmetry to criminal and avenger dying together. Don't cry. Why should your brother's life end up as three points and a paltry fine?

Get this into the papers. Start with the Echo then the nationals. Use the "Grieving Mum takes Desperate Measures" angle. The money is compensation for losing your brother and mother. Don't let your father or grandfather get it. They'll booze it away. You've got my spirit. Use it. As the mourning daughter of said desperate mum, who better to campaign against drunk drivers? It is vile to kill someone, cry in court and walk off. David won't bloody walk anywhere again.

Someone must take drink driving seriously. If any politician lost their children this way they'd get off their fat backsides and do something. I know, darling. I could stay and campaign. I could be with you. But someone must act for David. I've got the car and whisky. I'll drink quickly and get tanked up fast. I know where the useless b— will be tomorrow. I'll release my seat belt as I speed up to hit the rat. If the car doesn't kill him, I will as I go through the windscreen.

Everyone will think it was a tragic accident – a desperate mum loses control, gets drunk and unwittingly kills someone. The papers will like that angle. They will listen to the heroic mourning daughter. I'm covering everything for you, darling.

When you read this, I'll have played my part. Now do yours – for David, for me. You must. I've seen the rat's family. I heard the father claim our David got in the way of his son. Don't let the scum get away with it.

Name and shame the bloody lot with your campaign. Attack them. They mustn't get the chance to silence or intimidate you.

I know you can handle this. Go for the jugular, darling.

Love, Mum.

WHY STOP NOW?

I was born here, lived here, died here and stayed here, though my remains are in the cemetery two miles away. Why stay? This old-fashioned bungalow would be destroyed. Almost every other bungalow has been replaced by some monstrous mansion thanks to greedy developers. They're not getting this one.

You should've seen the reactions of the speculators when shown around by the estate agent as I howled, moaned and whined. How they paled when I made the curtains rise, windows and doors slam and household objects move at speed as I saw fit. When I "breathed" down these fools' necks, they all fled, ignoring the estate agent claiming it was the elderly central heating system playing up.

Humans have instincts for a reason. Perhaps estate agents have theirs sucked out with a straw. I'll give this guy his due. He kept bringing people round. Had his colleagues given him the short straw? I was pondering putting in an appearance to shift him as this farrago had gone on for months when he suddenly just left. I thought the drip-drip effect of continually driving his clients away finally worked.

I was wrong! The place was auctioned off. I confess I might've been careless to go on one of those Spectre Breaks arranged for those stressed out by too much haunting. When I returned a week later I was shocked to find a girl in my lounge. She was putting landscapes up. You don't do that to a place you'll knock down. I did wonder though why I couldn't have met this pretty, kind looking girl in life.

I followed her (though never in the bathroom or bedroom – a gent in life, I wasn't stopping now). She liked the same radio comedy I did, she read, cooked and kept flowers in most rooms. And when she died, I'd greet her, ghosts together.

It went wrong two months later. She began going out. I suspected she had a boyfriend. This was confirmed when one evening I saw a handsome male, about her own age I'd say, bid her goodnight at the door.

I scowled. This girl is mine. This house is mine. I will keep both.

She looked happy wandering into the house but she *would* be happy with me.

It was 2.00 a.m. when I went into the room with the pillow hovering in front of me. She wouldn't suffer. I told you I was a gent.

SO CLOSE

It has taken centuries to reach this point but you overcome anything to get what you crave. When I've drained one place of its prey, I move on but this predator crosses dimensions. I time travel sometimes (though it uses too much energy and right now I'm hungry so until I've topped up my food supplies I dare not risk it).

But the good news is I've found a sustainable food source. I need to break through this final barrier and plunder a new world full of delicious mammals. I'll attack the most intelligent forms of life. I absorb the finest qualities of my victims when I devour them, you see. And you think monsters only belong to fiction! Wrong, we do exist. You won't acknowledge it. It's harder to be top dog when something threatens you.

There! I've recited the transportation spell's last line. I am on my way. So when you go for a walk and feel your blood chill, it won't be due to Britain's permanently cold weather. Your gut instincts, the ones you suppress, will tell you there's danger. You'll tell yourself not to be silly, walk on and then die. And I will feed. If it's any consolation, I appreciate my food and any fine qualities it gives me. I expect to increase my ruthlessness genes when I absorb you.

Close. I'm so close now. The barrier opens. I can see where to go.

I can't wait to meet you.

EXPECTING

The old man's lifeless hand lolled down from the arm of his recliner.

Deborah Jones smiled. It wasn't a pretty smile. She shut the front door quietly. She'd left her red Astra a couple of streets away. Five minutes later, she drove off. All had gone better than planned. The old man wasn't surprised at tonight's visit, though he could never have predicted the outcome, given his treatment of Hannah and he said what he thought, just before he was strangled with his own woolly scarf. Hannah made it for the old git years ago.

Hannah will come round. It's not as if the old miser was grateful for all she did. I have set her free.

Deborah drove off, beginning to whistle, as ever, as she engaged second gear. Tonight's tune was *Always Look on the Bright Side of Life.*

It's not as if the neighbours will intervene. The old sod, when not driving Hannah round the bend, did that to the neighbours. I've carried out a public service here. I really have.

Deborah paused. The law would never see it that way despite moving on in other ways. There would be no obstacles to the relationship with Hannah now. Indeed they could marry. It was this thought which led the old git into calling his daughter names Deborah winced at when Hannah told her about them.

Deborah grinned as she approached the first of many roundabouts on her way home.

I'll be the comforting figure at the funeral. Then Hannah and I wander off into the metaphorical sunset.

That was the way it was meant to happen.

Instead, Deborah entered the bungalow quietly to find the old man's lifeless hand lolling down from the arm of his reclining chair.

Hannah's beaten me to it. Damn.

Careful to touch nothing not strictly necessary (and gloves ensured no prints were left), Deborah left the bungalow and scurried to her Astra. She drove towards the house Hannah recently purchased, thanks to an inheritance from her aunt, and where Deborah was to move into next week, her own house sale having finally gone through.

Deborah strode into the lounge. At this time, Hannah was usually watching a soap opera but the lounge was unoccupied. Deborah checked each room. No sign of Hannah. There were no notes. Hannah was meticulous about leaving notes or texting but Deborah's phone remained quiet and come to think of it, had done so for the last two days.

Starting to feel sick, Deborah went back upstairs and went to the drawer beside the double bed on Hannah's side. Hannah's passport was gone. Deborah checked the fitted wardrobe on the wall opposite the window. Hannah's clothes were gone.

Where the hell are you, Hannah? I don't understand. What have I done to deserve this? Why are you leaving me to carry the can?

GETTING IT RIGHT

The crone placed the shiny red apple in the wooden bowl.

Had that brat respected me as Queen, I could've removed her via a suitable marriage, but Madam rejected my friendship attempts. She likes wildlife. Now she discovers there is only one Queen in the hive.

The crone's reflection in the wisely silent talking mirror revealed her skin, usually smooth, was crumpled. The black robes were tatty. Her black hair was now greasy and lank. But get the girl's pity, she'd take that apple and die.

The crone smiled. It is because I'm worth it.

THE POISON PEN

She dipped her quill into the bottle of black ink and kept writing. Get one ingredient out of place or written down incorrectly and the spell would fail. Either the poison wouldn't stay in the apple or the fruit would glisten unhealthily which would warn any imbecile there was something wrong. Deception was key. The fruit had to be a healthy glowing red colour for just long enough for it to be consumed.

The crone stopped writing. There! The ingredients were in place. Now it was a question of locating them. She glanced around her extensive shelving which was crammed with every shape and colour of bottle imaginable. She had most of the items, she liked keeping good stocks, but if she knew anything from her years of being a practicing witch, it was that there would inevitably be things missing. She sighed, rose from her hard-backed wooden chair, and went to the nearest shelf.

There was one important factor on her side. The target of her special apple was an idiot and had no idea she had a rival for her husband. Get this apple down her and the woman would never realise. There had been rumours the so-called Queen and King were expecting a baby daughter so the crone had to act fast. *She* wanted power and besides she liked the look of the dark, handsome King, so it was time to act before it was too late. The King should be having children with *her*.

It was time to shop. There *were items* she needed. The opportunity to tackle the Queen would be approaching soon. The crone was determined to be ready. The Queen would die. *She* would be Queen. There would be no baby daughter with snow white skin, which is what the crone believed attracted the King to her rival in the first place.

The crone laughed softly as she wrapped her grey cloak around her and went out into the dusk. The King was going to need comforting after the death of his Queen and unborn child but the crone could do that. Sincerity, as with so many things, could be faked.

But first the apple…

One great thing once this ploy worked, the crone could destroy all evidence. It wasn't as if she would need to use it again.

PRESSING THE FLESH

It was 3 a.m.. The neighbours were sleeping. He must be quick. It was hard to disguise a cutter's sound but bodies didn't dispose of themselves. His ancestors knew that. They provided bodies for vivisection – animal or human, it didn't matter which. There were discoveries to be made. Science then was a hungry beast.

His market was different. So many could not afford the disgusting price of meat. So many could not afford to ask where cheap meat originated and instead were sensible and just ate what they could get.

TIME WAITS FOR NO MAN

It is almost time to go. I'm just waiting for the funeral cars. Time feels heavy. I've been expecting this moment for a long time but now it is here it feels unreal. Surreal almost.

Everyone says I'm handling the situation fine but they don't know what a bundle of nerves I am inside.

David died. The abusive David died because our mantelpiece clock was brought down on his head with considerable force. The clock is missing. The murderer would make sure of that.

I don't think anyone will ever find the thing.

REWARDS

She must go, Becky thought.

Becky paced her thick, red lounge carpet a dozen times. The beautiful Gemma had decided one boyfriend wasn't enough.

I've only ever dreamt of one man, unlike her. I can't reason with Gemma. She doesn't listen to other women. With her looks, why should she? Why are men so bloody gullible?

Becky returned to her chair and stared at the magnolia wall. She could see only one image. The mocking face of blue-eyed brunette Gemma Alderson, who was endowed with a bosom that could knock someone out if deployed as a weapon.

Becky sighed. Her brunette hair wasn't glossy. *Her* blue eyes didn't sparkle. Becky's bosom was adequate. Becky brought her clothes from *Bon Marché* and *Primark* but even if she could afford designer labels, she knew they wouldn't work on her the way they did with Gemma. No wonder the gorgeous Guy was giving Gemma the eye.

So help me, that will be all he gives her. I must stop her taking everything I love. Whenever I've mentioned the bloody woman, even Rosie wags her tail!

Becky frowned at the snoozing Bearded Collie lying at her feet. Rosie wagged her tail at the mention of almost anyone's name (unless they were named Kat).

Gemma treats other women as stepping stones. An accident will stop anyone asking

41

questions. The best murder is one where nobody knows it was one.

Becky reached for her half empty glass of *Baileys* and sipped at it. She grabbed her notebook from alongside her now empty glass, picked up her favourite pen (a big purple one that wrote in different colours though to date she'd stuck to blue and black) and jotted down ideas.

I'll plot this out before destroying these notes, but unless I write it down, I'll forget something crucial. Darling Gemma won't forgive lapses bar her own. It'll be straight off to the police if she suspects anything.

An hour later, just as the sun was setting, Becky finally smiled. It was good when a plan came together, especially one that would work.

You killed her.

Becky stared into her bedroom mirror. Her hair was all over the place, her blue eyes were bloodshot and her clothes were torn along the skirt hem and one arm of her white blouse.

You just did it. You look a mess. You've got form, Becky Wentworth.

Becky wondered how many could nag themselves *and* give themselves a headache.

So much for being cold-hearted enough to do the necessary, Becky thought. *I'm not cold-hearted enough to avoid feeling bad afterwards.*

Becky settled at her desk the following morning.

I must focus on work. I have masses to type up. Steve said he'd ring just after lunch to see how I'm getting on. At least I have something positive to say.

But it was funny how Gemma invaded Becky's thoughts whenever the latter decided it was time for cappuccino.

I should have guessed Madam wouldn't stay quiet, Becky thought. *Not that it matters. Gemma is still dead.*

The phone rang. Becky looked at her watch. Steve was five minutes late. 'Steve, good to hear from you.'

Becky listened to a deep disembodied voice and suppressed her urge to purr. Not only did Steve have a wonderful speaking voice, but whenever her agent rang to confirm another publishing deal, Becky was prepared to do more than purr. Perhaps she would drop Steve a hint later…

'That's wonderful news, Steve. I'm making great progress with *The Scarlet Woman*. I've finally got rid of Gemma! I can get this draft to you for next week.'

Becky listened to her agent again and gazed around her luxurious flat, all paid for thanks to Guy, her fictional detective. Not only did Becky write stories she loved, others liked them too, her books were beginning to do well and when she got a chance to murder a bitch, Becky saw that as a perk. Who said crime didn't pay?

THE OUTCOME

I'm pleased to be wrong about my misgivings.

There she is – the blonde in that sapphire gown dancing with the Prince. They look good together, don't you think? He's a nice, handsome boy, it's a coincidence *all* royals are good looking, and she's kindly, beautiful and deserving. I wish the rules would let me wreak overdue justice on her awful stepmother and stepsisters but the authorities would have my wand for that.

There goes Madam Stepmother to talk with the Palace officials. The daughters keep looking at the Prince. They want him to change his dancing partner. Not a chance! I didn't use a love spell. The Prince and Cinderella are attracted to each other without that interference. Good. I dislike using magic to make people fall in love. I know it's traditional but magic, to me, is for when there is no other choice and people should create their own happy endings.

Good. The officials have ushered Madam Stepmother away. She doesn't look happy. Excellent. The music has stopped. The Prince and Cinderella have gone out to the gardens. I'd better ensure my goddaughter doesn't do anything she'll regret later. It's all very well for promises to be made but he *will* damn well keep them. Everything must be done by the book. It's never the bloke's reputation that gets ruined...

Ah, they're walking in the rose garden. Too busy looking at each other. I check my watch. It's 11.59 p.m. What are the chances of my goddaughter remembering she must be away by midnight? Remote I should say. If he cares, he will follow when she runs off. The Palace clock above the stables begins to chime the hour. Cinderella panics. Good. She's left a shoe behind. His Nibs has picked it up and is pursuing her, waving it, but he has no chance of catching her. Cinderella always was good at running and won her school's sports day races four years in succession.

My job now is to ensure Sunny Jim aka the Prince does try the "I'll marry the girl whose foot fits this slipper" routine. I've programmed the shoe so it can only fit Cinderella though I wasn't happy with how the spell worked. The shoe was meant to be a fur one. I still don't know why it ended up being made of glass. I urged Cinderella to be careful. I wouldn't fancy wearing glass. It's bad enough getting bunions. At least it doesn't matter what the stepmother does now. That is the main thing.

It's a day later and I'm in the Big Brother house… er… sorry… Palace Grand Hall and the announcement has been made. The Prince will marry the girl whose foot fits the slipper. Good. Job done. This will play out nicely. You just see if it doesn't.

PEN PORTRAIT

Mary brushed her hair once a day whether she needed it or not, following Shirley Williams' school of thought rather than Margaret Thatcher's. Mary's clothes and shoes would've seen her through a battlefield. She walked a Bearded Collie that was equally windswept.

Mary's make-up was minimal, only wearing some to prove she had feminine attributes. She hid the obvious ones under a jumper that would conceal Dolly Parton's bust. Nobody would guess she worked as a stripper gram. That suited Mary just fine. And it saved embarrassing the vicar next door.

MY LIFE

It is all white dresses, lace and flowers now but I hated him when I first saw him. I am not just saying that. He was *such* a snob.

But then I find he helped my silly sister. Yes, Lydia, the one who ran away with that unscrupulous rogue, Mr Wickham. I thought *he* was charming when I first met him. I have learned not to judge by appearances now. It clearly was a lesson I needed to learn.

Anyway I looked at the man who is now my groom in a new light after his help here. You would, would you not?

Am I pleased to be Mrs Fitzwilliam Darcy now? Oh yes. I could never have just married anyone. And I like to think I have moulded him. He and I should get along just nicely now he has got rid of his pride and I have removed my prejudice.

CHANGING MY MIND

I do not know why changing the mind should only be the right and privilege of a woman. I do not accept that.

I was wrong about her. Plain and simple. I thought she must be like her foolish relations, especially her sister, Lydia, but *they* would not have challenged me the way *Elizabeth* did. *They* would have kept me happy knowing I am wealthy. *Elizabeth* told me exactly what she thought!

My name? Since you ask, Fitzwilliam Darcy. And I must say my bride, Elizabeth, looks wonderful as she walks down the aisle.

The best thing? After the celebrations she and I can escape. Escape from her family and my snobbish aunt. None of them see honesty and truthfulness is far more valuable than wealth or breeding. I now know who the fools are. Elizabeth and I are not amongst them.

HELPING OUT

It's not every day you untangle Hanacrill, a fairy who, Merlin knows how, got caught in a Leylandii hedge but being a witch means being able to handle anything though I'm not meant to rescue fairies.

Hanacrill, who should've looked where she was going, rescued me from a dragon and her boss, the Fairy Queen. Anyone can miss a dragon (some are subtle hunters, they're not all huge and blazingly obvious) but I should've spotted the fairy monarch given she's the one person who cannot go anywhere without her squad of trumpeters so she has a fanfare ready to go.

Hanacrill is the Kingdom's top performing fairy (I wonder what the others fly into) and I'm the best witch next to my boss. She frightens everybody. Even the Queen avoids confrontation with her. Says she doesn't want war. She doesn't want to risk losing, more like it. Probably doesn't want to lose her trumpeters either. During the last magical war many of the Queen's musicians perished. The Witch's granny considered them an easy target. If all you've got to defend yourself with is a big bass drum, she has a point. The British on earth organize this better. Their military musicians are soldiers first, musicians second.

It is a custom here on the prelude to war between fairies and witches the best of each are put into direct combat as a "warm up". Hanacrill and I are not thrilled. I've found it easier to build a friendship with my "rival" than with my colleagues. Hanacrill said the same after thanking me for cutting her down. She said it was because we *weren't* competing for jobs or status. We know we're on opposite sides and that's that. So she and I decided we must work together to avoid that direct combat scenario. I think I've got the answer though goodness knows what Hanacrill will make of it.

I guess you call it helping out. You do what you must to stay out of trouble. Hanacrill is due any minute. Her boss will welcome her visiting me as much as my boss would. A whoosh of wind comes from my right. Hanacrill always did like appearing in a blaze of glory. I wait for her self-created dust cloud to vanish, and watch my sparring partner head towards me.

'What is it, Griselda? What do you want?'

If anyone tells you fairies are gracious, forget it. They can be as grumpy as anyone else.

'Top of the morning to you too, Hanacrill. I summoned you because I've found a way to stop us having to fight one another.'

Hanacrill brightened. 'What is it?'

I beam at her. 'We run away. I know you've got no answer to that.'

I was right. She hadn't.

YOU NEVER KNOW

So you think I live a luxurious life as a tour guide? That I stay in the poshest hotels, sleep in the finest beds (alone before you ask), dine on the finest food and enjoy the best wines and all for free?

You're right. I do. There is a price though.

Stop scoffing. I can hear you. Magical beings have sensitive senses, even junior class fairies like me.

The problem with being a tour guide is you never know what your clientele will be like. It's all very well when they're nice but that is far from the case at times.

Some lap up everything you say, others contribute useful historical knowledge while the rest show-off and are a pain in the butt. Sadly those are the ones with the most money so you shut up. You quickly learn when tact pays.

Incidentally have *you* tried being rational with an out-of-sorts orc? *I* have. Given they haven't got the sunniest of dispositions at the best of times, even you should appreciate that is not easy. So stop whinging I have it easy. I *can* hear you muttering.

Attitude is everything here. It is not always clear who is the powerful wizard or the meddling apprentice. I assume anyone I meet could blast me to smithereens if I cross them. It's a sensible approach. It limits how likely I am to offend someone (and die for doing so).

Even if the clientele behave themselves, they all want to see the volcano where that troublesome ring was dumped. Some idiot always tries to fish the thing out again. We have to take the same route that heroic hobbit took. It's in the contract. Don't follow that to the letter and you're out on your ear and other parts of your anatomy before you can blink. I've seen that happen.

I don't mind sushi during that tour (or the Gollum Special as we call it) but it is not for everyone. I couldn't see you tolerating it. I heard your crack about my gobbling everything edible. Okay so I have put on weight, I am a dumpy fairy, but I must try the food. It's in my job specification. So there. It's also the best way of convincing the clientele they will be looked after. You won't risk your own life eating something dodgy after all.

One further tip to the wise – never eat anything glowing red as it's unlikely to be healthy. I must thank Snow White for telling me that. *She* should know so do listen to her, even if you ignore mine.

Now tell me again, are you sure *you* want to be a magical tour guide?

THE SELFISH FAIRY

Once upon a time struck Eileen as twee, as did the usual fairy names, which was one reason why she ditched hers years ago, picking something nice, drab and human to irritate her cousin, the Fairy Queen. Humanity equalled war and pollution.

Eileen caused scandal by pointing out loudly the magical realm wasn't much better. Many areas in the Fairy Kingdom were barren thanks to having too much magic go through them during the wars. She'd written her version of magical history and knew damned well it was only her royal connections that stopped her being arrested for writing "wrongly" and enabled the book to be published, albeit with numbers forcibly kept down. Every copy of the book was purchased by the government and installed in the Palace library where anyone could ask permission to visit. Nobody did. Eileen knew they'd need nerves of steel.

There was no better way in the government's eyes of being instantly marked as a troublemaker. The magical world's ways of dealing with them involved expertly applied pain.

So Eileen spent most of her time fighting dragons and other foul creatures. She was also renowned for her favourite curse, which was to turn someone into a frog, leave their mind untouched so they could figure out what happened, and then dump them in the middle of a heron colony. When she fancied a change, she turned them into a toad. The Kingdom's herons had never been so well fed. Eileen was never troubled by old enemies haunting her.

Nor did Eileen go in for the standard fairy costume. There was no way in any dimension anyone could name she'd wear the frilly pink tutus fairies were expected to wear. Eileen wore fleecy separates. The wind got into awkward places when flying. Eileen liked her comforts. She'd been condemned via the Fairy News Network bulletins for her attitude here but was still puzzled as to why. For her it was common sense to wrap up warmly when flying. Still the Queen had finally stopped complaining about Eileen's improper dress. Eileen had fought for years for the right to wear trousers and won. Feminism took many forms.

Eileen's attitude was also considered wrong when dealing with the Chief Witch, cousin to the Queen and Eileen. Eileen was of the "let's get together and talk" school of thought for dealing with the crone, whose favourite activity was to turn up at important christenings uninvited and curse the unfortunate babe with death by spinning wheel. Eileen always cancelled this out though she was still looking for something better than the 100 years sleep option. To date, Kingdom "scientists" had failed to come up with a spell that could overcome the Witch's curse. This was another area where Eileen vehemently complained and unsurprisingly that did nothing for her popularity either. The Queen and her government sought to destroy the Witch, an attitude Eileen pointed out was bound to get right up the nose of anybody, only to be accused of appeasement. The Witch never attacked

Eileen, despite the fairy godmother being her obvious rival. Eileen saw this as proof her attitude was correct. The Kingdom saw it as Eileen's "reward for sin". If Eileen wasn't so useful in destroying the foul creatures the Witch sent, Eileen knew she'd face treason charges. Good fairies weren't supposed to do that.

I'm not a good fairy then, Eileen thought.

Eileen looked at her handsome reflection in her Palace bedroom mirror. It didn't talk. It could but it would be a foolish inanimate object that did the usual "cheery" routine with Eileen. She smashed objects that got on her nerves and word of that behaviour spreads.

I'll do. Time to battle ogres again. The Witch must like using them so much as they're one of the few creatures uglier than she is. Poor love. I must tell her to moisturise more.

Eileen grinned. She liked having a talent to annoy. Good fairies weren't supposed to relish that either. It was all duty, duty, duty.

Not for me, Eileen thought. *I'll enjoy my career or dump it.*

Now it was time for more fun. Not for Eileen the happy ever after. But the happy for now and the blast evil creatures to bits routine suited her nicely. She strode out of her bedroom. Household staff shrank back against the plush walls as she made her way to the Palace's outer doors. Nobody sensible got in Eileen's way. She liked that too.

RAISING THE STAKES

I can't see why you're upset. He may have been your hero but he was a multiple killer. *You've* been taken in by all his glamorous images. I blame the films and a certain Sir C. Lee, late of this parish, for that.

Someone has to stand up to evil somewhere along the line. Did you really want us all to become like *them*?

No? I rather thought not so get out of my way. My name is Van Helsing. Someone has to raise the stakes and I know exactly what to do with them.

MAKING THE GRADE

I did it. I showed them all. They said I never would. Doom merchants the lot of them. They were wrong.

I passed my magical exams with a whopping 90% pass rate. Neither did I cheat. That did come as a disappointment to my mother but I am from a long line of witches where cheating in magical practice comes as naturally as breathing.

Still as I told Mother, if this is what I can do when I'm honest, just think of the possibilities when I'm not!

A STUDY IN MAGIC

She expertly extracts revenge, dispatching man and beast where necessary. She dresses well though despises fashion slaves. Her long brunette hair, gleaming in sunlight, is her vanity. She doesn't "get" jokes. Humour gets in the way for the Fairy Queen's exterminator of evil.

Only fools cross Deamadrell. She uses her own adaptations to her world's ancient spells. Her favourite is to turn an offender into a frog, ensuring they stay fully aware of what happened, before dumping them in a heron colony. Nobody complains.

The Kingdom's herons have never been so well fed.

TELLING THE TIME

I inherited the beautiful grandfather clock, aptly, from my grandfather. He swore it kept better time than Big Ben. I tried telling him that was the name of the bell but he was having none of it.

Much as I miss my grandfather, part of me is glad he isn't around to see his wonderful clock has gone horribly wrong. It has not been the same since that mouse got into the workings. Instead of chiming the hour, the bloody thing squeaks now.

On the plus side, I always know when it is 1 o'clock.

THE MINT WITH A HOLE

Never trust anyone who says something can't be done. Someone somewhere will rejoice in proving you wrong. Reading my paper, I must admit I can't help but admire the brass nerve of some people for their daring and initiative. Clearly they can't take "impossible" as an answer.

In medicine they'd come up with wonderful cures, in literature they'd write fantastic fiction, in sport they'd set new world records but what to achieve if the category you're aiming for is crime?

You do what the people I read about did. You rob the Royal Mint!

HEALTH AND SAFETY

I don't know why people are moaning. I was road testing products – everything from furniture to food and I gave my opinions on them all. I left whatever I didn't like. Now that is a review.

Breaking the chair was accidental but I'm not heavy and it should've been made to a better build standard. It was an accident waiting to happen. Is there any gratitude I literally took the fall? Not a bit of it!

As for that horrible porridge, Baby Bear is better off without it. Since when do bears feed on oats anyway?

THE MADMAN

Just because I like to come up with ideas that might help improve the lot of my people, they think I'm odd. I like to think they feel threatened by my ingenuity. I keep that thought to myself. There's a limit to how often I like to be mocked. It becomes tiresome.

And they laughed at me again an hour ago. Okay this time I concede they've got a point. My idea does have a design flaw but I know what to do.

Instead of inventing a square wheel, I should have come up with a round one.

THE CIRCLE OF LIFE

People throw kittens into the river here. I hate that. It's so cruel. What can I do?

I thought I'd rescue the poor animals but they'd only be thrown in again when I'm not about. I know my people. Subtle they are not.

So I decide to create a need for cats. If people need them they won't drown them so the kitties win as well. How to do this? Easy peasy.

Get all the mice I can find and unleash them on the village! I'll be setting the first lot free at dawn.

ANIMAL PARADE

The animals went in two by two.

The crowds stared as different species entered Noah's boat as if it was the most natural thing to do. Perhaps the animals knew something. Maybe Noah *wasn't* mad for making a boat miles away from the sea.

The crowds left once the parade finished. A crowd needs a show. The show was over. There was still no sign of a cloud yet alone rain.

Nobody spotted the cockroaches, woodworm and fleas that hid amongst the fur and feet of the other creatures to book *their* place on the Ark.

SHE DID IT HER WAY, KIND OF

Jane Westbrook knew it was too late to do anything. Tomorrow, someone else could live with Harry's misdemeanours.

'There are people who can help, Jane.' Mary Randall said after finishing her carrot cake. 'You can get rid of Harry. People would rather you'd admit it wasn't working. Then *they* can sort him out.'

'I love Harry but he's driving me nuts, Mary. After having me up during the night every night for the last ten days, I've had enough. There has been no real reason to disturb me. It's not as if I can lie-in.'

'You would…'

'Don't say it, Mary, please. It's what my mother says. She's never had time for Harry but he is a good soul.'

'He's not ill?'

'Harry is only ill is when off his food. And he isn't!'

'You just left him?' Mary sipped her coffee and watched as Jane remembered she too had a drink.

'Harry knows I must go out sometimes. He saves his behaviour issues for my return.'

'Typical male behaviour, yes?'

Jane managed a smile.

*

Within two minutes of being back in her semi-detached chalet, Jane wished she'd stayed at the café. She didn't know how Harry had done it given she'd put the box on a high shelf but tissues were all over the hall and two cushions had bitten the dust.

'Harry!'

Harry didn't respond. She wasn't surprised.

To Harry's surprise Jane remained silent after that call. He wasn't sure he liked that. He was less keen when she left the house *again* ten minutes later. He'd rather have had Jane's lecture and moved on. If he could ensure she'd do as he wanted, then everything would be fine. She wouldn't want to get rid of him. Jane knew William. William died. Harry didn't want to be alone again so that meant staying with Jane. But it had to work. It wasn't looking great right now. And how else could he get her attention?

'I thought you were getting tougher with him,' Mary said, putting the cafetière aside to brew and retrieving two huge mugs from a mug tree. Mary wasn't sorry Jane was visiting, albeit unexpectedly. She'd been urging Jane to visit. And there was always time for coffee.

'He looks at me and I weaken. I'm hoping my walking out whenever he does something wrong might wake him up.'

'Jane, do you expect Harry to understand? He's a Springer Spaniel!'

'He's a very intelligent dog.'

'Yes, intelligent enough to run rings around you. How old is he now?'

'Nine months.'

'Have you thought of obedience classes?'

'Who for – Harry or me?'

Mary laughed. She was pleased Jane smiled too. Harry was a wonderful companion after Jane's boyfriend, William, was killed in that car accident but Harry was now trying to rule the roost. Jane needed to retake control – of her dog, her house and her life.

Harry noted his mistress was smiling.

'Forget the walk, Harry. I must tidy first. If you weren't so messy, I wouldn't have so much to do.'

Harry's tail stopped thumping the floor. He disliked tidying. It meant the vacuum came out. Jane would only scold him again if he resumed barking at it. He couldn't do anything right. Not now William had gone. Harry whined.

When Jane switched the vacuum on, Harry hid under Jane's bed. It was a while before she saw the dog again, peering out with sad eyes.

My hero, Jane thought.

Harry bolted out and ran downstairs. Jane laughed. She didn't laugh when she put the vacuum away and found Harry in the kitchen bin, scattering rubbish everywhere.

Jane screamed.

The dog barked.

The doorbell rang.

'I'm not selling, Madam,' the young man began.

Jane said nothing. How many times had she heard this?

'Could I interest you in…?'

Jane began to shut the door when Harry emerged and cocked his leg against the would-be salesman's cheap pinstriped trousers.

Jane giggled.

The young man swore and ran up the street. It was the only option since berating the owner of an untrained puppy wouldn't achieve a sale either.

'Well done, Harry!' Jane patted the dog's head.

Harry woofed. It was time his mistress told him he was doing something right. Maybe they would be okay. William would have been the one training him. Harry guessed he'd have to settle for Jane's way of doing things. He could live with that. Now he knew she could.

GEORGE CHANGES HIS MIND

He refused to kill the dragon. Not this one. Not after last time. The girl he'd rescued from the other monster screamed for so long he'd wished he hadn't arrived in the nick of time.

All George wanted was a quick thank you and maybe a peck on the cheek. But no, the girl had to have hysterics. George sighed. Being the good guy sucked. And he was tired of being a sucker but now he had his chance…

The dragon had not seen him, George would swear to that. None of the villagers gathered around the rock where *another* screeching girl was tied to await her fate had spotted him. George knew he should feel ashamed. He watched the dragon approach the girl and…

To everyone's surprise, the dragon flew up and above the screaming "maiden" (George had his doubts on that qualification, he'd heard the rumours and there were *lots* of those).

To George's horror the dragon landed in front of him on the hill behind the village.

George went for his sword.

'Hold it right there, sunshine,' the dragon said. 'I just want a breather. I've had a trying morning. I'll leave shortly. I won't kill you. Show me the same professional courtesy, please.'

'Weren't you supposed to…?'

The dragon snorted. 'Eat *that*? I just couldn't face eating *that* screeching harpy. I think they're getting desperate. I've heard rumours about that one. If she's a virgin, I'm turning veggie. Can you imagine the indigestion she'd have given me?'

THE HAUNTING

The bloody thing *is* there!

I could've sworn I left it at Waterloo Station. If ever there was a place to lose something you didn't want to see again, it's there.

I swear it's haunting me.

I laughed at Gran when she said the thing haunted her. She tried dumping it in the sea. The waves came back in and shoved the thing at her feet. She tried again. Same thing happened. She gave up after a dozen attempts. Said she was fated to keep it.

Shame really. It's the ugliest umbrella *ever*.

SANDBAGGING

I'm sick of being patronized. I'm not elderly where that's an occupational hazard. I said this to the suited idiot canvassing my vote but I may as well have talked with the man in the moon. This wretched MP allowed some Council moron to sell off a therapy centre for the elderly. I was told it's called budget management. I said it's called mugging the elderly.

I asked the idiot if he realised how stupid it is to give elderly folk occupational and physiotherapy sessions for six weeks for chronic conditions when most need a little exercise often and permanently. What happens when the six weeks are up? Their joints seize up again. Where will they go if these centres close? He could only bleat about needing to keep costs down. I just know if his elderly relatives needed help they'd get it. Why can't we peasants have the best care too?

It was fun stunning this idiot. A nice mum isn't expected to sound off. With this idiot I had the set. The Tory chap went blue in the face, the Labour lady blushed but I let the Liberal Democrat off. Looking yellow is never good.

TIME WAITS FOR NO MAN

But time does slow to a crawl when driving in traffic. Time speeds up for anyone in a queue, say at the bank, and their bus is due.

Karen Granger sighed. Time could be a vicious beggar but today would be different. She knew her bus would not go without her.

I drive the flaming thing, she thought. *My poor passengers must wait. As will I. I seem to be in the middle of a bank robbery. Of all the times I could've picked to just stop off and pay in a cheque...*

COMING UP ROSES

I was brought up by dear old Mum to show appreciation for help given along the way.

I've made friends because I say thank you with chocolate. All I do is check if the recipient is diabetic first but most aren't.

I've been in hospital recently. My asthma has been under control so the worst attack I've had in years took me by surprise, but I've had so many cards and good wishes my usual way of thanking people won't work this time.

There's a limit to how many Cadbury's *Roses* boxes I can carry!

Printed in July 2019
by Rotomail Italia S.p.A., Vignate (MI) - Italy